MILLIE AND THE MOUNTAIN

A SHORT STORY

ALEXANDRIA BLAELOCK

BlueMere Books
MELBOURNE, AUSTRALIA

For permission requests, please contact
enquiries@bluemerebooks.com.

Ordering Information:
Discounts are available on quantity purchases. For details, contact orders@bluemerebooks.com.

Millie and the Mountain/Alexandria Blaelock
paperback ISBN: 978-1-922744-33-3
digital ISBN: 978-1-922744-34-0

MILLIE AND THE MOUNTAIN

The day we moved into our new home was bright and sunny.

Not one of those crisp and cold sunny winter days, but the kind with the soft, warm sunlight that wraps itself around you like a big blanket.

Which was lucky, because the carpets were damp and stinky from whenever the previous owners steam had cleaned them.

How lucky we were to have the doors and windows wide open for long enough to dry the carpets and dissipate the smell before it set in.

And lucky too to have a tiled kitchen big enough to stack all our boxes so they didn't need to wait outside or touch the carpet.

The outside air was tinged with the eucalypt scented woodsmoke drifting lazily across the wire fence from our new neighbour's chimney.

A couple of Magpies clutched the power line as they welcomed us.

Crimson Rosellas peppered us with questions from the naked pear tree.

We were very excited - this was the end of our youthful nomadic existence. It was time to stay in one place and put down a root or two.

For a while anyway.

When we signed the purchase contract, we made a pact to stay there, in that house, at least until the dog we hadn't bought yet died.

Say 15 or 20 years.

We were excited about that too.

Not that there's anything wrong with using your employer's greed to travel the world, but in the end, it gets a bit tiresome learning new cultures and languages.

And making new friends only to leave them a couple of years later.

So, we'd tossed a coin, and David's "home" won over mine, and here we were.

Setting up a new home of our own, back in Australia.

Back in the land he'd grown up in, though he'd been away for so long he didn't really know it anymore.

In any case, we hadn't gone back to my sleepy home town; that would have been like getting off an express train while it was still moving.

And we'd chosen Melbourne over Sydney, because it reminded us of the European cities where we'd been happy, rather than the American ones where we hadn't.

Plus, it's not called the Coffee Capital of Australia for nothing!

While we waited for out belongings to arrive, we took a driving holiday round Victoria.

We visited the sandstone ridges and kangaroo mobs of the Grampians, the wide wilderness beaches of Wilson's Promontory, the Goldfields of Ballarat and drove along the Great Ocean Road to Portland.

We were looking for a place we fit.

It's funny, the Australian Aboriginal Nations believe you belong to the land, not the other way around.

That no matter where your people come from, the land you're born on, is your home. And the people who live there, are your people.

That's why it's so important their remains are buried in their country - so their spirits are reborn among their people.

Not that I know a lot about it, but it feels to me, as though the land chooses you.

That it calls and calls until you come to it.

And so it was for us.

We'd gone for a drive through the forests of the Dandenong Ranges National Park.

We'd walked through Mountain Ash trees as tall as City buildings and under ferns almost as tall, drinking in the smell of damp ground and foggy air.

The light streaked through the forest canopy as we held hands, gazing into each other's eyes, standing as still as if we too were deeply rooted in the ground.

All around us wild birds called, and wild creatures rustled in the undergrowth.

We felt the sacred spirit of the land calling us home.

Leaving the Park, we got lost.

And in the best tradition of fairy stories, found ourselves up a dead-end street facing a darling white weatherboard cottage.

It was old, and in bad condition, but it combined all the best features of all the holiday houses we'd visited during our travels.

It was perfect.

When we got back to our rented apartment in the City, we started looking at real estate websites, and wonder of wonders, there was the very same cottage.

Listed that very day.

As if it was meant to be.

Just like the land was calling us home.

We put an offer in the next day, and the day after that, we signed the purchase contract.

The cottage seemed enormous compared to the tiny apartments we'd been living in.

I think you could pretty much fit the one we left in the cottage's lounge.

We didn't know how we'd ever fill it with stuff.

Once we understood how they worked, the large double hung windows, helped cool the house on scorching hot days, as did the copse of gum trees it nestled within.

Not that gum trees are the best for shade, or for the structural integrity of your home, but if you want to live with the sound of birdsong, you have to live in their habitat.

The covered merbau decking was perfect for our new tradition of evening cocktails watching the sunset, and talking about our days.

And when Millie the golden Labrador finally arrived, it was the perfect spot for her to snooze in the morning sunshine or afternoon shade.

Watching the road and waiting for us to come home.

And the mailman.

Labradors have the reputation for hearty appetites, and Millie was no exception. It was a constant struggle to keep her weight down.

One of her favourite treats was possum poo, sucked up as hors d'oeuvres during her morning ablutions.

She also liked fresh fruit, stripped directly from the tree by taking a long run up the yard, launching herself into the air, grabbing a branch in her jaws and letting gravity do its work.

Oddly, after a few half-hearted attempts at catching a bird, she gave up on them.

Perhaps she realised they were good guides to what in the garden might be worth eating at different times of year.

Or perhaps they ganged up on her and introduced her to the consequences of killing their young.

All in all, she was a cheerful and well behaved, if bossy dog.

But, as it turned out, despite our morning walks, she regularly let herself out and took long walks around the neighbourhood on her own.

We only found out when we got home from work one day to find the gates closed, and a note from our neighbour telling us that she'd "rescued" Millie during one of her perambulations.

That night we got out the torches and crawled around in the undergrowth, looking for her escape route with no success.

The next day, our neighbour had contained her in the front garden again, so I put a bucket of water in there for the time after that.

We checked the fence line again, this time shaking it and pulling at the assorted boards, panels and wires it was made up of, but still no sign of her escape route.

Mind you, she was following us around the fence, so perhaps she'd successfully distracted us at the crucial moment.

Clever girl!

But it did mean one of us had to stay home to see how she was escaping, so I negotiated with my boss to work from home for a day.

It turned out to be a very productive day for me, I got a lot done without the day-to-day distractions of telephone calls and useless colleagues.

But, not a successful dog escape detection day.

Millie, had a delightful and restful day indoors sleeping under my desk while I worked.

I kind of liked it, even if it didn't advance the cause.

But it seemed it was enough to turn the corner.

For a while, she was contentedly waiting in the back yard for us when we got home from work.

We thought the situation had been contained.

We were mistaken.

Not that we can blame her.

Dogs are descended from wolves, and wolves roam in packs.

A dog, left on her own all day, is bound to wander looking for something to hang out with.

We started to notice things like leaving a clean dog when we left home in the morning, and finding a filthy one when we got back.

Or that some days she was almost too tired to eat.

Or that she'd be limping.

One Summer evening we got home, and she wasn't there.

We called, and she didn't come.

We kicked her food bowl around the deck, a cue that had always worked in the past, but she didn't come.

Cicadas mocked us from the trees.

We were worried.

Grabbing her lead, we climbed the hill into the National Park, rattling it and calling her name.

It felt like we roamed for miles and miles, for hours and hours, but I'm sure it wasn't that long.

Eventually, we heard her yelp, so we knew she was near.

We kept looking, and finally found her, lying in a large hole nestled in some tree roots.

A half-eaten creature of some kind lay nearby.

She thumped her tail once, and whimpered breathily.

She didn't even try to get up.

She was filthy.

She'd vomited, she'd lost control of her bowels, and she was lying in it.

We thought she'd probably eaten the creature. And that it was either decomposing or had died from some kind of poison.

Regardless, it'd made her ill and we had to get her to the vet as quickly as possible.

David is fitter than me, and has longer legs, so he bolted back to the house to get the car and a blanket.

I collected the dead creature in a poo bag in case the vet wanted to test it or something.

Hoping she could walk, I tried to roll Millie out of the hole and onto her feet, but just succeeded in rolling her over.

She didn't have the strength or inclination to get to her feet and walk.

Her healthy appetite meant her 33 kg body was too heavy for me to lift, if I was going to move her, I had no option but to drag her.

Across the stony ridge and down the hill towards the closest place we could meet David and the car.

Snagging her body here and there on tree stumps and branches.

Would we get to the vet any quicker?

Maybe a little.

Would she be better or worse off with road rash as well as poisoning?

I was afraid worse, but I couldn't just sit and wait for David to return.

Deciding my t-shirt would offer Millie some protection, I took it off and started wrapping it around her body.

She whined as I manhandled it underneath her and tied the sleeves across her chest.

Then I grabbed her front legs and start pulling her towards me.

She was fine for a little while, but soon enough she was trying to pull free of me.

We rested for a bit, and then we were off again.

It seemed like forever before David arrived with the blanket.

We wrapped her up like a sausage and carried her to the car.

David took off for the vet with a squeal of tyres.

I'd forgotten I wasn't wearing a top until we rushed into the surgery, and the waiting pet owners looked at us curiously.

The vet nurse kindly gave me a scrub top to wear.

We sat on the hard seat waiting for a vet to see us, cradling Millie on our laps, stroking her head and patting her swaddled belly.

She wasn't chafing at the restraint, and we thought for sure she was a gonner.

They took Millie away to see to her, and we waited, even though they told us not to.

Taking it in turns to pace up and down the waiting room, even though they'd told us to go home.

Stinking up the place and getting in people's way, even though they said they'd call as soon as they knew anything at all.

Waiting as the sun set.

Waiting while the nurses gossiped, smelling their dinners, and until our bums lost all feeling.

We waited, and waited.

And then waited some more.

A burst of light, and noise, and movement, and we were in the recovery room with Millie.

She was clean, sedated, and hooked up to a drip.

She was going to live!

It seemed as though the land had claimed her too, and kept her safe within its soil until we could collect her.

While she was in dog hospital, we had all the fences replaced so she couldn't escape again.

And once she'd recovered, we took her to a local dog shelter to choose a new friend she could stay home with.

Now she's always on the deck waiting for us when we get home.

THE END

ABOUT THE AUTHOR

Alexandria Blaelock writes stories, some of them for *Ellery Queen's Mystery Magazine* and *Pulphouse Fiction Magazine*. She's also written four self-help books applying business techniques to personal matters like getting dressed, cleaning house, and feeding your friends.

As a recovering Project Manager, she's probably too fond of sticking to plan. She lives in a forest because she enjoys birdsong, the scent of gum leaves and the sun on her face. When not telecommuting to parallel universes from her Melbourne based imagination, she watches K-dramas, talks to animals, and drinks Campari.
At the same time.

Discover more at www.alexandriablaelock.com.

BOOKS BY
ALEXANDRIA BLAELOCK

SHORT STORY COLLECTIONS

The Histories of Hayward Hall
Lovelorn, Lovestruck and Love at First Sight
Common or Garden Variety Heroes
Case Files of the Wilkinson Detective Agency
Unavoidable Fates
Christmas Travesties
Five Faces of Felicia Clarke

OTHER FICTION

That Love Nonsense

MS BLAELOCK'S BOOKS

Stress Free Dinner Parties
Signature Wardrobe Planning
Holistic Personal Finance
Minimally Viable Housekeeping
Planning a Life Worth Living

SELECTED SHORT STORIES

Alma's Grace
Balancing the Book
Carmelita Basingstoke
Fate in Your Hands
Kiss of Death
Lady of the Looking Glass
Life in the Security Directorate
Long Weekend in the Snow
Love in the Past Tense
Love in the Security Directorate
Morning Star, Evening Star, Superstar
Needy Bitch
Payton's Run
Phoenix Child
Secret Singer
Shining Star
Ship in a Bottle
Simone Says Hands in the Air
Special Relativity in Space
The Bygone Boyfriend
The Day the Schedule Broke
The Ghost Detectors
The Guardian's Vigil
The Mince Pie Mystery
The Mystery of the Master Suite
The Pseudonym's Bride
The Shadow Thieves
The Time-Space Paradox
Toy Soldiers